nilo and the tortoise

TED LEWIN

SCHOLASTIC PRESS • NEW YORK

Nilo is pronounced Nee-lo.

Panga is Spanish fisherman slang for dinghy, a
small boat that is towed behind a bigger boat.

ISBN 0-590-96004-0

Copyright © 1999 by Ted Lewin. ● All rights reserved. ● Published by Scholastic Press,
a division of Scholastic Inc. ● *Publishers since 1920.* ● SCHOLASTIC and SCHOLASTIC PRESS and
associated logos are trademarks and/or registered trademarks of Scholastic Inc.

LIBRARY OF CONGRESS CATALOG NUMBER: 98-27489

10 9 8 7 6 5 4 3 2 1   9/9 0/0 01 02 03 04

Printed in Mexico ● 49 ● First edition, May 1999

The illustrations in this book were painted in watercolors. ● The display type was set
in Impact. ● The text type was set in Goudy. ● Book design by Marijka Kostiw

This book is dedicated

to my guide,

william,

to

captain fausto,

and to the

crew of the poderoso.

—T.L.

ar, far away, on the other side of the world, is a place like no other . . . a place where volcanoes released their lava to make tiny islands that are homes to many animals but few men.

And on one of these islands, so far, far away, is a child like many others, a child who loves animals and adventures. His father, a fisherman, needed to repair the engine of his boat, so he anchored near an island. Now, everyone knows that it's not much fun to be on a fishing boat while your father is making repairs. So the fisherman and the child packed some fruit, then went by panga to the island.

Once the child, whom we know as Nilo, had his fill of play, he began to search the shore for his father's boat. Let's join him.

Standing on the black, rocky beach, Nilo saw sea lions, their
heads bobbing in the surf, and, beyond them, the vast empty sea.
But his father's boat was nowhere in sight.

Nilo walked among the rocks, where he found the anchor. Holding its broken line, Nilo knew that his father's boat would be swept out to sea and that much time would pass before his father would be able to get help and return for him.

There was only one thing for Nilo to do. Explore.

A frantic bark jarred Nilo from his thoughts. He looked

into the angry, whiskered face and sharp teeth of an enormous

sea lion.

Nilo ran—not the swift and joyful run of play—but the heart-thumping run of fear.

"No more! No more!" he shouted. "I'm going now!"

After the bull had retreated, Nilo followed an old lava flow up the volcano. Then he stopped.

Nilo was attracted by a happy chattering. A tiny red and black bird danced in the air, then perched on a branch. Though Nilo came close to the bird, it did not fly away.

"If I had wings like yours, I could fly high in the sky to look for my father, but since I don't have wings, I will climb to the top of the volcano to look for him," Nilo said. "Good-bye, little bird."

As Nilo climbed, the air cooled. A wind-born mist wrapped
the boy like a wet sheet, and he could not see where he walked.
His feet slid back over the loose lava soil as he climbed the steep
volcano. Still wrapped in thick mist, he finally reached the rim.

Nilo walked along the rim until he suddenly emerged from the mist and found himself in warm sunlight. Looking down into the deep crater, Nilo felt like a tiny mite on the rim of a giant soup bowl.

A large bird flew overhead. It came closer and closer, settling upon a lichen-covered tree. Nilo looked into the yellow eyes of the hawk and wondered if those eyes had seen his father's boat.

No matter. Nilo was hungry. He curled up under a bush and
ate a banana from his bag. Hearing a great hiss, Nilo looked up to
see a giant tortoise, thick-legged, with drops of water dripping
from its mist-wet shell, and neck extended as if listening to voices
in the sky.

A tiny finch, then another and another, found the tortoise.
Nilo watched as they made a meal of the ticks that had been
feeding themselves on tortoise blood. Nilo approached.

The boy reached out and pulled a tick from the tortoise's head. The tortoise extended its neck and waited for more.

Nilo ran his fingers along the smooth plates of tortoise shell.
The urge to climb upon the great domed back proved to be
irresistible. With his ear pressed against the shell, he could hear
hissing sounds coming from within while the tortoise grazed.

As the sky grew dark, the tortoise dug a shallow hole in the ground. Nilo helped. The tortoise settled into the bed, and Nilo, feeling sleepy and safe, settled next to it.

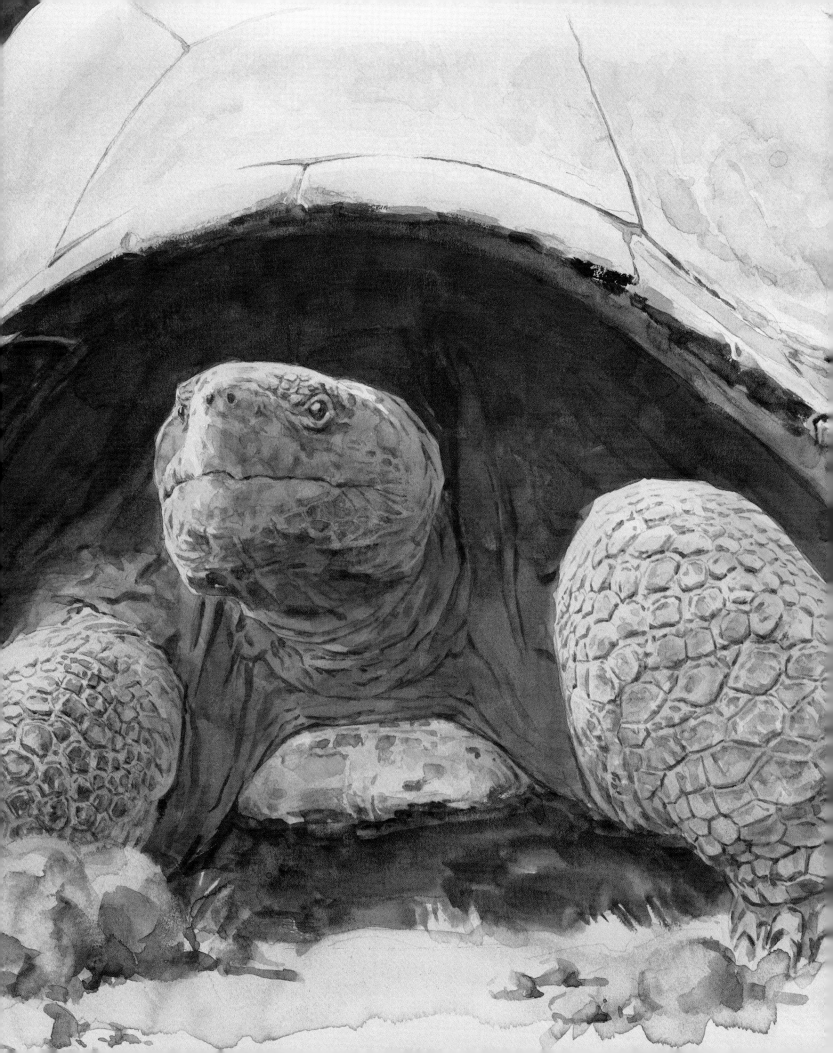

Awakened by the screaming hawk, the boy knew it was time to go. Nilo fed the old tortoise the rest of his fruit, then said good-bye.

Walking down a steep, dusty path, he followed the hawk to the beach where his father was waiting.

giant tortoise

The giant tortoise can weigh up to six hundred pounds and live more than two hundred years. It feeds on grass, leaves, flowers, and the prickly pear cactus. Ticks that feed on the giant tortoise are then eaten by finches. Flies that feed on tortoise droppings are then eaten by birds and lizards. Four thousand giant tortoises live on Alcedo Volcano.

darwin's finches

Thirteen species of finches live on the Galapagos Islands. Each species has its own characteristics and its own song.

california sea lion

Sea lions live in herds. Within the herds are groups of females and pups and a bull sea lion who aggressively guards his territory. Sea lions can be very playful and may swoop in close to you when you are swimming. California sea lions live along the coasts of California, Japan, and the Galapagos.

galapagos hawk

Though similar in appearance to the red-tailed hawk, which is found throughout the United States, the Galapagos hawk is found only on the Galapagos Islands. Unlike other hawks, the Galapagos hawk will not flee when approached by humans. Both male and female take part in raising the young. This behavior is rare in hawks.

vermilion flycatcher

A resident of the southwestern United States and Central and South America, the vermilion flycatcher is also well established in the Galapagos Islands. The male is red and black and the female is brownish gray. The vermilion flycatcher feeds on insects caught in mid-air. It has a song of rapid, twittering notes.

GALAPAGOS ISLANDS

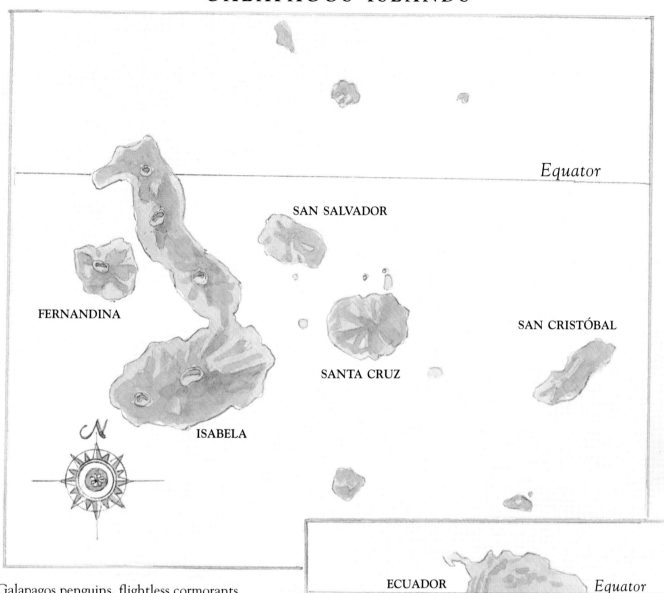

Equator

SAN SALVADOR

FERNANDINA

SANTA CRUZ

SAN CRISTÓBAL

ISABELA

ECUADOR

Equator

GALAPAGOS ISLANDS

SOUTH AMERICA

Galapagos penguins, flightless cormorants, Galapagos fur seals, and marine and land iguanas are also found on the Galapagos Islands along with many kinds of sea and land birds, lizards and snakes, and geckos and bats. Dolphins, orcas, humpback whales, and green sea turtles abound in the surrounding sea.

Humans first discovered the islands in 1535 and brought cattle, donkeys, goats, pigs, cats, and rats. The newly introduced species threaten the delicate ecology of the islands' indigenous animals. The five largest islands are Isabela, Santa Cruz, San Cristóbal, Fernandina, and San Salvador.

dear reader,

This story was inspired by a visit I made to the Galapagos Islands. They lie in the Pacific Ocean, six hundred miles off the coast of Ecuador. The animals that live there have no fear of man. Some of them, like the giant tortoise, are found nowhere else on earth.

In telling the story, I tried to recreate some of my experiences on Isabela Island, where I fled an angry bull sea lion, watched vermilion flycatchers dance, made the hard climb up Alcedo Volcano, shivered in the cold mist, and was awed by the enormous caldera. A hawk hovered just above my head. Spellbound, I watched finches groom a giant tortoise; that night, I slept near the tortoise. The next morning, I returned to the beach to find my boat dead in the water, in need of a battery.